Hello, Family Members,

W9-CDD-568

Learning to read is one of the most important accomplishments of early childhood. **Hello Reader!** books are designed to help children become skilled readers who like to read. Beginning readers learn to read by remembering frequently used words like "the," "is," and "and"; by using phonics skills to decode new words; and by interpreting picture and text clues. These books provide both the stories children enjoy and the structure they need to read fluently and independently. Here are suggestions for helping your child *before*, *during*, and *after* reading:

Before
- Look at the cover and pictures and have your child predict what the story is about.
- Read the story to your child.
- Encourage your child to chime in with familiar words and phrases.
- Echo read with your child by reading a line first and having your child read it after you do.

During
- Have your child think about a word he or she does not recognize right away. Provide hints such as "Let's see if we know the sounds" and "Have we read other words like this one?"
- Encourage your child to use phonics skills to sound out new words.
- Provide the word for your child when more assistance is needed so that he or she does not struggle and the experience of reading with you is a positive one.
- Encourage your child to have fun by reading with a lot of expression . . . like an actor!

After
- Have your child keep lists of interesting and favorite words.
- Encourage your child to read the books over and over again. Have him or her read to brothers, sisters, grandparents, and even teddy bears. Repeated readings develop confidence in young readers.
- Talk about the stories. Ask and answer questions. Share ideas about the funniest and most interesting characters and events in the stories.

I do hope that you and your child enjoy this book.

—Francie Alexander
Reading Specialist,
Scholastic's Instructional Publishing Group

If you have questions or comments about how children learn to read, please contact Francie Alexander at FrancieAl@aol.com

For Dr. A.D. Shapiro,
who helps kids fight germs
— B.K.

To all the wonderful people
at Shepherd of Peace Preschool
— S.B.

Special thanks to Dr. Lawrence Golub for his expertise.

No part of this publication may be reproduced in whole or in part, or stored in a retrieval system, or transmitted in any form or by any means, electronic, mechanical, photocopying, recording, or otherwise, without written permission of the publisher. For information regarding permissions, write to Scholastic Inc., Attention: Permissions Department, 555 Broadway, New York, NY 10012.

Text copyright ©1998 by Bobbi Katz.
Illustrations copyright ©1998 by Steve Björkman.
All rights reserved. Published by Scholastic Inc.
HELLO READER, CARTWHEEL BOOKS, and the CARTWHEEL BOOKS logo
are registered trademarks of Scholastic Inc.

Library of Congress Cataloging-in-Publication Data
Katz, Bobbi.
  Lots of lice / by Bobbi Katz; illustrated by Steve Björkman.
    p. cm. — (Hello reader! Level 3)
"Cartwheel books"
  Summary: In rhyming text, head lice, or "cooties," explain how they like to invade schools and live in children's hair and reveal how they can be stopped.
  ISBN 0-590-10834-4
  [1.Pediculosis—Fiction. 2. Lice—Fiction. 3. Stories in rhyme.]
  I. Björkman, Steve, ill. II. Title. III. Series.
PZ8.3.K128Mg 1998
[E]—dc21
                                                                97-27254
                                                                     CIP
                                                                      AC

10 9 8 7 6 5 4 3 2 1   8 9/9 0/0 01 02

Printed in the U.S.A.   24
First printing, September 1998

LOTS OF LICE

by Bobbi Katz
Illustrated by Steve Björkman

Hello Reader! Science — Level 3

SCHOLASTIC INC.
New York Toronto London Auckland Sydney

Do you like insects that are cuties?
Then you'll love us.
Meet the cooties!

No one knows just how many
lice could fit on just one penny.

We're little guys.
We don't have wings.
But oh, how we can
louse up things.

Folks call us cooties.
But actually,
     LICE
is the name on our family tree.
     LOUSE
is the name for just *one* of us.
Like mice and mouse.
No muss. No fuss.

Cooties have one golden rule:
To get a-head, invade a school.

Lots of lice know school is where
lots of lice find lots of hair.

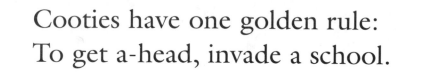

All lice are small.
Yet in spite of our sizes,
each branch of the family
    specializes!

Lice like us bite,
but some cousins might chew.

If they live on birds,
that's just what they do.

Lice live on plants,
fish,
and *almost* all mammals.

But the lice
found on rats
aren't quite like those
on camels.

So cooties don't live just anywhere.
We're lice that live in human hair.
We've been on earth for years and years.
We brought the ancient Greeks to tears.

Some of us were even found
on mummies that were neatly bound
in Egypt many years ago.
Now that's a nifty fact to know.

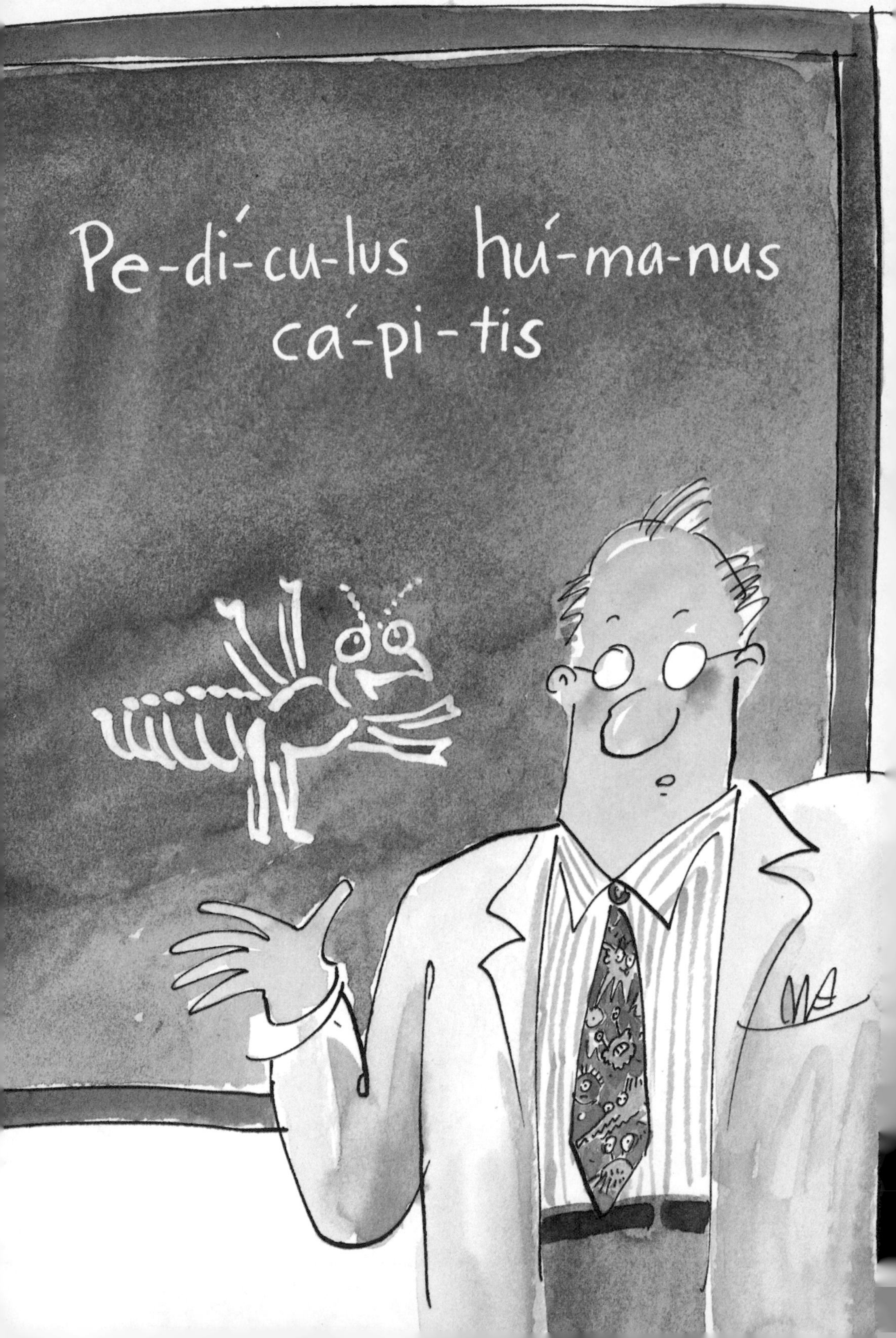
Pe-di´-cu-lus hu´-ma-nus
ca´-pi-tis

Scientists thought it would be nice
to give big names to different lice.
  Pediculus humanus capitis—
that's the name they gave to us!

In Latin *capitis* means "head."
A finer word was never said.

Three cheers for heads!
Why? Heads grow hair!
And cooties glue their eggs right there.

Our oval eggs are known as nits.
And nits can give your school nurse fits.

In six to ten days, the nits will hatch.
Soon they'll lay another batch.

Our soft mouths are shaped like beaks
to sip your blood for several weeks.

Then we're ready — hair by hair —
to lay more eggs with loving care.

Before we do, we crawl with glee
from head to head so merrily.
Cooties think it's only fair
that kids in school should learn to share!

So don't be selfish. Lend! Lend! Lend!
Pass those headphones to a friend.
Lend combs and brushes, helmets, too.
Help lice to visit ALL of you!

Living cooties
are hard to see.
Light always makes us
hide and flee.
Where do we hide on
you, my dears?
Check the back of
your neck.
Check behind your ears.

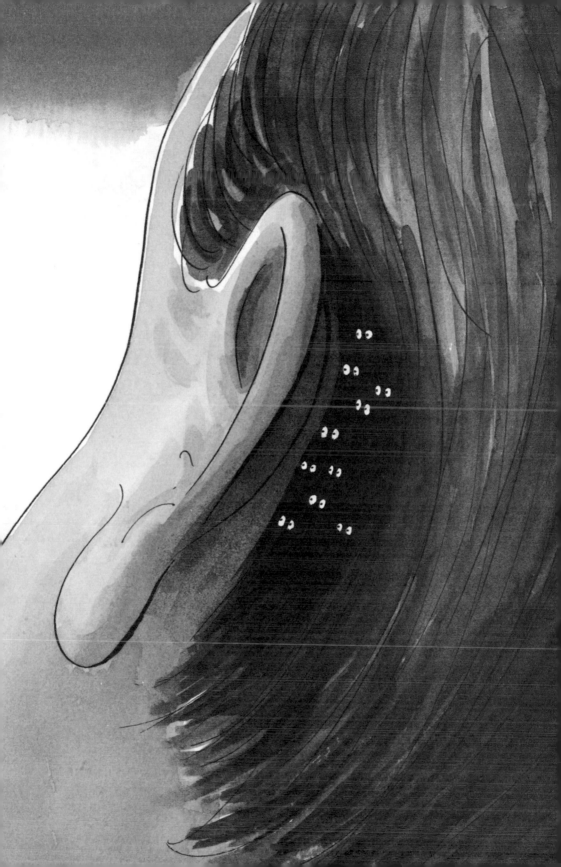

Cooties are easy for you to catch.
You'll itch, itch, itch,
     and
scratch, scratch, scratch!

We're little guys.
We don't have wings.
But oh, how we can
louse up things!

One thing that every cootie hates
is when a school cooperates.

Families working together
can stop our show.
Please, Nurse, don't tell the P.T.O.!

Families working together
house by *house*.
How would YOU feel
if YOU were a louse?

Sucked up on loose hairs
with a vacuum cleaner —
our poor little nits!
What could be meaner?

Special lotions and shampoo
can zap live cooties.
Sad but true.

Nit-pickers combing head by head
can make sure that our eggs are dead.

Boiling, steaming
hats and combs
spoil our chances
to get new homes.

Wrapped in plastic
for a rest in the cooler.
Frozen headphones!
What could be crueler?

Good people, hear the cooties' plea:
DON'T ACT LIKE A COMMUNITY!

Fix one kid here . . .
            and one kid there.
Cooperation is not fair.

Although we drink your blood,
it's true,
there's plenty more
inside of you.

Respect the cooties' golden rule:
To get a-head, invade a school.

Lots of lice know school is where
lots of lice find lots of hair.

We're little guys. We don't have wings.
But oh, how we can louse up things!